Carlos & Carmen

The Big Splash

by Kirsten McDonald
illustrated by Fátima Anaya

Calico Kid

An Imprint of Magic Wagon
abdobooks.com

For Jesse Figuera who launched Carlos and Carmen with a big splash —KKM

To my sister Gabriela, thank you for everything. —FA

abdobooks.com

Published by Magic Wagon, a division of ABDO, PO Box 398166, Minneapolis, Minnesota 55439. Copyright © 2020 by Abdo Consulting Group, Inc. International copyrights reserved in all countries. No part of this book may be reproduced in any form without written permission from the publisher. Calico Kid™ is a trademark and logo of Magic Wagon.

Printed in the United States of America, North Mankato, Minnesota.
052019
092019

Written by Kirsten McDonald
Illustrated by Fátima Anaya
Edited by Bridget O'Brien
Design Contributors: Christina Doffing & Candice Keimig

Library of Congress Control Number: 2018964632

Publisher's Cataloging-in-Publication Data

Names: McDonald, Kirsten, author. | Anaya, Fátima, illustrator.
Title: The big splash / by Kirsten McDonald; illustrated by Fátima Anaya.
Description: Minneapolis, Minnesota : Magic Wagon, 2020. | Series: Carlos & Carmen
Summary: The Garcias are enjoying the afternoon at the pool until Carlos gets water in his eyes, but when it seems like the fun will be over, Carmen figures out how to let everybody have a splashing good time.
Identifiers: ISBN 9781532134913 (lib. bdg.) | ISBN 9781532135514 (ebook) | ISBN 9781532135811 (Read-to-Me ebook)
Subjects: LCSH: Hispanic American families--Juvenile fiction. | Twins--Juvenile fiction. | Brothers and sisters--Juvenile fiction. | Swimming--Juvenile fiction.
Classification: DDC [E]--dc23

Table of Contents

Chapter 1
Ready to Go

It was a hot day. It was a sunny day. It was a great day to go to the pool at the park.

Carlos and Carmen raced down the stairs to the kitchen. Mamá was slicing apples and cheese. Papá was filling water bottles.

"¡Mira, Papá!" said Carmen. "We have on our swimsuits."

"¡Mira, Mamá!" said Carlos. "We have towels for everybody."

"We're listo!" the twins said together.

Mamá and Papá added the food and water bottles to the swim bag.

"And we've got the snacks ready," said Mamá.

"Then what are we waiting for!" said Papá. "¡Vámonos!"

Just then, Spooky popped out from under the kitchen table.

"Murr-uhhh?" she asked.

"No, Spooky," said Carlos. "You can't come with us."

"Cats don't like swimming," Carmen added.

"I know something cats do like," said Carlos. He got the apples out of the swim bag. He pinched off four pieces and put them in Spooky's dish.

Spooky swished her tail and ran to her dish.

"Now we're all listo," said Carlos.

"Then, like I said," said Papá.

"¡Vámonos!"

Chapter 2
Into the Water

At the pool entrance, people were selling things. One person was selling ice cream. One person was selling giant pretzels. And, one person was selling all sorts of things for the pool.

11

Carmen looked at Carlos. Carlos looked at Carmen.

"Are you thinking what I'm thinking?" they said. And because they were twins, they were.

"Can we get helado?" the twins asked.

"We'll see about ice cream," said
Mamá.

"Can we get pretzels?" they asked.

"We'll see about pretzels," said
Mamá.

"Forget about helado and pretzels,"
said Papá with a laugh. "Let's see
about getting wet."

The Garcias hurried through the gate to the pool. They put their things on chairs next to a big umbrella. The twins raced to the edge of the pool.

"¡Mira!" Carmen shouted.

She jumped into the pool and sank to the bottom. Then she burst back up with a big splash.

Carlos sat on the edge of the pool.
He slipped into the water with no
splash at all.

"Bet you can't catch me!" Carmen
shouted to her twin.

"Bet I can!" Carlos shouted back.

Carlos reached out to get his sister. Carmen ducked underwater and swam away. She popped up, and Carlos lumbered through the water toward her.

Carmen ducked underwater again. She zipped through the water away from her twin.

Carlos really wanted to catch his twin. But, she could swim faster than he could walk.

He squeezed his eyes tightly shut. He pinched his nose tightly closed. Then he went under the water.

It was hard to swim using just one arm. And, it was hard to catch Carmen with closed eyes.

Carlos stood up in the water. He wiped his face several times with his hands. Then he cautiously opened his eyes.

"¡Mis ojos!" Carlos shouted. He shook his head and swiped at his eyes. "I have water in mis ojos!"

Chapter 3
A Wet Problem

Carlos sat on the edge of the pool. He kicked his feet in the water. He made sure the splashes did not go near his eyes. Carmen popped up in front of him.

"What's wrong?" Carmen asked.

"I want to go under the agua like you," said Carlos.

"¡Mira!" said Carmen. "Just go like this." She splashed down to the bottom of the pool. When she popped up, she said, "You can do it."

Carlos gave his legs a little kick. He said, "But I don't like getting water in mis ojos and in mi nariz."

Carmen thought for a minute. "Yo sé," she said. "You can swim with your eyes closed."

"Then I can't see where I'm going," said Carlos.

"Hmm," said Carmen, and she thought for a while. Suddenly, she said, "Yo sé. You need goggles!"

"Goggles would be good." Carlos smiled. "They'd keep water out of mis ojos." Then his smile faded. He said, "But, I'd still get water up mi nariz."

It was a problem. A wet, splashy, in-your-face problem.

After a minute or two, Carmen shouted, "¡Yo sé!"

She climbed out of the water.

"Where are you going?" asked Carlos.

"It's a sorpresa," said Carmen.

Chapter 4
The Surprise

Carmen walked over to their chairs
with the big umbrella. She whispered
something and pointed to Carlos.
Mamá and Papá whispered back.

Then Papá gave Carmen something, and she dashed away from the pool.

"Where's Carmen going?" Carlos shouted.

"It's a sorpresa," Mamá and Papá answered.

A few minutes later, Carmen came back to the pool. She was hiding something behind her back.

She walked over to her twin. She said, "I have a sorpresa for you."

"What is it?" Carlos asked.

"Hold out your hands and close your ojos," Carmen said.

Carlos squinted his eyes shut and held out his hands.

Carmen placed a swim mask in her brother's hands. She said, "¡Mira!"

Carlos opened his eyes. He looked at the swim mask. A big smile lit up his face.

"Will it work?" Carlos asked as he put on the mask.

"There's one way to find out." Carmen grabbed her twin's hand.

They had smiles on their faces.
They had sparkles in their eyes.
And, one of them had a swim mask
strapped to his head.

"Ready!" said Carmen.

"Set!" said Carlos.

"¡Vámonos!" they said together.

Then, they jumped in the water with
the biggest splash ever.

Spanish to English

agua – water

helado – ice cream

listo – ready

Mamá – Mommy

Mi nariz – my nose

¡Mira! – Look!

Mis ojos – my eyes

Papá – Daddy

sorpresa – surprise

¡Vámonos! – Let's go!

Yo sé – I know